The Emperor's Underwear

ORCHARD BOOKS
96 Leonard Street, London EC2A 4RH
Orchard Books Australia
14 Mars Road, Lane Cove, NSW 2066
ISBN 1 86039 423 X
First published in Great Britain 1996
First paperback publication 1997
Text © Laurence Anholt 1996
Illustrations © Arthur Robins 1996
The right of Laurence Anholt to be identified as the author
and Arthur Robins as the illustrator of this work has been
asserted by them in accordance with the Copyright, Designs
and Patents Act, 1988.
A CIP catalogue record for this book is available from the
British Library.
Printed in Great Britain

The Emperor's Underwear

Written by Laurence Anholt
Illustrated by Arthur Robins

ORCHARD BOOKS

There was once a country where no one wore any clothes at all.

It was a very sensible thing to do. There was no washing, no ironing, no mending, no folding, no putting away, no dressing or undressing.

So there was plenty of time for really important things, like climbing trees and doing handstands and dancing about in the sunshine.

All through the summer it was the happiest country in the world. Without their clothes, everyone was treated alike – big or small, rich or poor.

Even the Emperor was just like an ordinary
person, without a crown or fancy clothes.

In fact, people spent most of the day laughing out loud, because everything seemed so funny.

After all, even strict Headmasters aren't very frightening in their birthday suits.

Of course, there were no uniforms either. So when the police chased the robbers it was hard to tell one from the other. They all got into such a muddle that they just fell about laughing.

There was no doubt about it – in summer, it
was the happiest country in the world. But
in winter . . .

. . . that was a different story all together. All through the winter, the icy north wind whistled around the streets until every bare botty turned blue with cold.

One particularly chilly morning, the Emperor woke up with goose pimples all over his royal body. The wind moaned around the palace . . .

. . . and the Emperor moaned around the
palace, too.

He jumped up and down and rubbed his
hands together, but by breakfast time even
his goose pimples had goose pimples.

All morning the snow fell, and throughout the land people stayed indoors and shivered like blueberry jellies.

Then, at lunch time, there was a knock at the palace door. In came two strange men.

The Emperor could see straight away that they had come from a different country because they were wearing CLOTHES! But being a kind Emperor, he tried not to laugh.

"Good day, Your Noble Nakedness," said the first man, stamping the snow from his boots.

"Greetings, Oh Royal Rudeness," said the second man, brushing the ice from his woollen hat.

"We are tailors from a distant nation," they said.

The Emperor wasn't sure what a tailor was,
but he smiled and shivered politely.

"We have come to make you the most beautiful bloomers in the world to keep your royal bottom warm," they announced.

"What?" said the Emperor. "Me? Wear knickers? You must be joking. I have to set an example to my people, you know."

"Yes, yes, Your Beautiful Bareness, but these are not ordinary pantaloons, they are MAGIC KNICKERBOCKERS, because they will be completely INVISIBLE to the naked eye (if you'll pardon the pun).

No one will be able to see them at all – unless they are a complete banana brain, that is!"

"Amazing!" said the Emperor, his teeth chattering a bit more.

"Mind you," continued the tailors, "magic undies don't come cheap. You will have to start us an Underwear Account at the bank so that we can buy all the magic wool we need."

So the tailors moved into the palace. Night and day, and day and night, they cut and stitched and sewed and made, not one pair of underwear, but hundreds and thousands of pairs in every shape and size.

There were Y-Fronts and Y-Not Fronts, and Boxer Shorts and Thermal Long-Johns and Purple Posing Pouches and Itsy Bitsy Teeny Weeny Yellow Polka Dot Bikinis and Woolly Winter Warmers and even Leopard Skin Tonga Thongs.

34

Of course, the Emperor and everyone at the palace could see *exactly* what they were doing, but no one said a word in case people thought that *they* were complete banana brains.

At last the tailors brought the Emperor a pair of Y-Fronts and a woolly vest, all extra large size.

The Emperor allowed the tailors to help him squeeze into them.

"Oooh!" he said, " they're all nice and warm – even though I can't see them!"

The Emperor was so pleased with his new underwear, he hopped onto his bicycle and went for a ride around the town.

When he had gone, the tailors began to
laugh and rub their wicked hands together,
"Snee hee heee!"

The Emperor rode proudly backwards and forwards along the High Street and although it was still snowing, a large crowd gathered to watch.

Of course, everyone could see the royal underwear perfectly well, but they didn't want anyone to think that *they* were silly old banana brains, so they said nothing at all; only clapped and cheered as the Emperor pedalled by.

All of a sudden, a tiny boy who was shivering on his father's shoulders pointed his little cold finger at the Emperor and shouted:

"Shh!" hissed his father. "That's the Emperor, and he's not wearing anything!"

"Oh yes, he is!" shouted the boy. "Dat man wearing nice warm woolly panties. Me want some woolly panties too!"

"The Emperor is wearing panties,"
someone whispered. "The Emperor's
wearing underwear!"

"Yes!" everyone shouted. "The Emperor's wearing underwear and WE WANT SOME TOO!"

The Emperor turned all red inside his white woollies and pedalled back to the palace.

"I really am a big banana brain, " he sighed. "Whatever have I started?"

In no time all, the wicked tailors opened a big underwear shop in the High Street and people soon began queuing outside.

It wasn't long before everyone started wearing underwear. Some people wore socks too . . .

. . . and trousers and shirts, and even ties on Sundays.

And of course, it wasn't long before they had to spend all their time washing . . .

. . . and ironing . . .

. . . and putting away.

Although the people weren't cold anymore, they didn't laugh quite so often. Policemen looked like policemen, teachers looked like teachers. . .

. . . and the Emperor looked so important in his royal clothes that nobody spoke to him anymore. He began to feel very lonely and fed up.

One hot day, in the
middle of summer,
when everyone was
sweltering in their
woollen clothes, the
Emperor decided he
had had enough.

He pulled off his
royal robes and his
crown and hopped
back onto his bicycle.

Then he rode proudly up and down the High Street carrying a large sign. It said . . .

And on the back it said. . .

All the people turned out to clap and cheer.
Then they began to pull their clothes off
too!

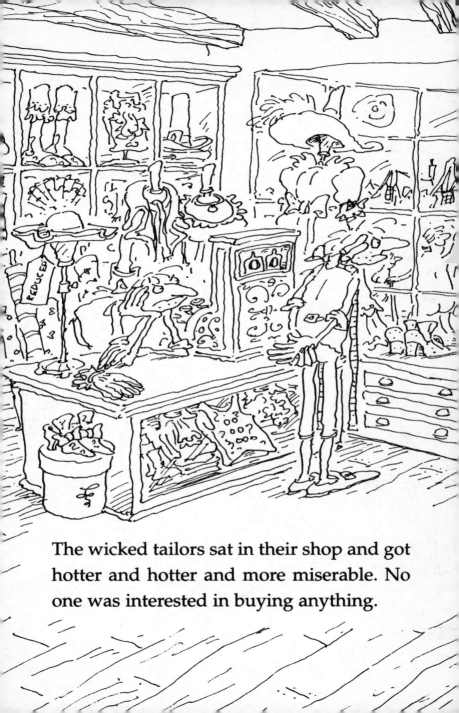

The wicked tailors sat in their shop and got hotter and hotter and more miserable. No one was interested in buying anything.

In no time at all everyone was laughing
again – just as they had before.

Soon even the tailors joined in. They set up a stall selling suntan lotion and ice lollies instead.

But the person who laughed loudest of all was the Emperor himself.

"Perhaps I am a banana brain," he chuckled. "But I'm a big, bare, happy, old banana brain!"

And he cycled away into the sunshine.